PUPPY SCHOOL

David Dayan Fisher

PUPPY SCHOOL

David Dayan Fisher

ISBN 987-0-578-06095-8

Illustrations by Kurt Hartman

Manufactured by Bookmasters Inc.
30 Amberwood Parkway
Ashland, OH 44805
Date Manufactured: Jul 2010
Job # : D5916

Typesetting by WORDZWORTH®

www.wordzworth.com

The Author

David Dayan Fisher is a British actor, who moved to Los Angeles nine years ago, from London, to make his dream come true. His determination paid off, and he has since acted in hit Hollywood movies, and TV shows ranging from National Treasure, The Librarian, 24, and has now been a regular guest star for four years, on the hit show, NCIS, as the CIA agent Trent Kort.

He loves his acting, and he also likes to paint, write and take photos. But his real love is of his two dogs, Burton and Monkey.

"This story came to me in a dream. It is meant to be. It has to be told".

Introduction

I was having dinner with some friends one night, and one of their dogs was misbehaving.

"He needs to go to Puppy School!" I said, jokingly.

That night, in my sleep, in one long dream, the story of Puppy School came alive, like a movie.

Even when the dream ended I knew I would not forget it, so I continued in my sleep with a big smile.

The next morning I woke up and wrote down the story.

Most of the characters are based off real dogs and people I know.

I dedicate this book to my mother, my family, and especially my niece and nephew, Pebbles and Louie. And to the dogs who inspired the story: Percy, Perry, Chimp, Cowboy, Harley, Jack, Burton and Monkey.

Because of my love for dogs, I would like to donate a large percentage of the book's income to dog rescue and dog pounds, and do all I can to assist in helping other abused animals.

If you have a dream, if you want to make something of your life, you must always follow your heart and never listen to those who doubt you or put you down. Dreams do come true. This book is living proof.

Pedigrees and Mutts: An explanation.

In the dog world there are mutts and there are pedigrees. But there are many types of pedigree dogs: Golden retrievers, Labradors, Great Danes, Husky, German shepherds, poodles, Chihuahuas, and many more.

When a golden retriever has puppies with another golden retriever, this is a pedigree. When two different types of pedigree dogs have puppies they are mutts. Quite simple. A mutt is a mix of two that are not the same. Yet if you read this story, there will be a truth, and a secret revealed that changes these very facts.

The story of a dream that became a reality.

Chapter 1

In the countryside, in a place, somewhere in this world, there is a wonderful farm called Sunnyfields. The sun has just started to peek over a hill that shelters the farm. Under a big oak tree at the top of the hill sits Jack – a chocolate colored Labrador dog. Jack is not old and he is not young. He is a very proud and calm dog. His coat shines and his eyes glint. He is the kind of dog you know you can trust.

Below him is the wonderful Sunnyfields Farm. It has a nice big red barn and a timber farmhouse with smoke drifting out of the weathered brick chimney. On a pond in front of the house, ducks and geese, enjoying the brisk temperature of the morning, quack and flap their wings.

Twisting through the farm like a snake is a small stream with tall reeds that line its banks and dance in the wind. On the other side of this stream there is an old rickety barn and windmill with a much smaller, older farmhouse. All around the old house there are

rusty farm machines sat like statues with weeds and grass growing all around them. The morning song of the birds is in full swing, and the rabbits scurry around for their breakfast.

Inside Sunnyfields' red barn, at the back, there is a small wooden fenced off area full of playful pedigree Labrador puppies. Some are black, some are yellow, and one is chocolate. This chocolate lab, which we will soon get to know, has a spirit and curiosity unlike any of the others. This is Burton.

As the puppies play, a beautiful, grown-up, golden Labrador glides into the barn. This is Wendy, their mother. She is the perfect looking dog in every way: her nose is as black as ink, and her golden coat is so shiny, it looks as soft as silk. As she walks in, proud as can be, all the puppies stop their play and rush up towards her, excited, yet all very well behaved.

"Soon you will be off to Puppy School to learn to carry our name forward with pride," Wendy says. "You will go into the world and become a breed of class and quality, trained to the full extent of your pedigree. You will be put into the finest homes, with the top quality of humans. Puppy school is not easy. It is where only the finest of dogs go." Just as she finishes her little speech, she notices the chocolate puppy, Burton, chasing his tail. He has distracted himself and forgotten to pay attention. She stops and looks over at him spinning around and around, mouth open, trying to catch his catch. All the other puppies turn to see their chocolate brother as he finally snaps his mouth closed on his own tail. They try not to chuckle. Burton not only catches his tail, but he tugs it so hard he pulls himself over. Some of the other puppies can't hold their giggles in anymore. Wendy looks at him. They all look at him. Burton – now with his tail in his mouth – looks up and sees everyone is watching him.

Wendy shakes her head. "As I was saying, the finest of our breed – the top pedigree," she says, smiling.

Burton spits out his tail and a few extra hairs from his mouth. "Sorry, mum," he whispers shyly.

Meanwhile, across the stream, outside the old barn on the rickety farm, a group of mutt puppies are playing. They are a bundle of mixed up colors, not one of them pure like the pedigrees across the stream. One of the puppies that seem to stand out for no real reason is Monkey. His coat of brown, black, and white is like an accident in a paint factory. As the others play nearby, Monkey trots over to his mother, Harley, and asks, "Mama, why is it we don't go to puppy school?"

All the other mutt puppies stop what they are doing. Their mother laughs. "Puppy School? You're just a mutt, Monkey. You go where you are taken, and you do as you're told, and that is that. Our types don't belong there. Just forget any foolish notions of mixing with those sorts. We are what we are," says Harley.

Monkey hears, but he still does not understand. All the other puppies start making fun of him, strutting around with their noses in the air, walking tall, and pretending to be pedigrees.

"I'm Monkey. Sir Monkey to you," says one of the pups. "I was born with a silver bowl, a gold collar, and a diamond leash. Be gone with you, you mutty mutts. I am Monkey, the pedigree!"

All the other mutt puppies roll around laughing. Monkey smiles and stands tall. Harley looks at him with a little sadness. He holds his head up even higher and walks towards the stream, confident in his belief. He looks back at his brothers and sisters, and then at the big, red barn across the stream. A little hint of fear comes into his eyes, and he shrinks a little as the words of his mother echo in his head: "Our types don't belong there."

Monkey shakes his head and shakes out the doubt. He looks back at his family, then back at the red barn. Then, with a determined leap, he jumps down the bank, across the stream, and up the other side. He runs under some farm machinery, across the grass, hops up onto a crate, and onto a barrel that sits next to it by the side of the barn. From here, he has a clear view into the window.

Inside, all the pedigree pups are groomed and their coats glimmer as the morning light bursts through the barn doors. Monkey looks at them, then down at his own shabby paint-splattered coat.

Wendy stands in front of all the pups, which sit in a row like little puppy soldiers. "Tomorrow afternoon is the start of your journey to greater things in life. You should be as proud as I am to be who you are.

Tomorrow is Puppy School!" she says proudly.

All the pups bark and cheer. Monkey sits, and thinks. Suddenly, as if a big light bulb has been turned on in his head, he jolts up straight and his eyes light up. He has an idea. He rushes down off the barrel, across the grass, under the machinery, and leaps across the stream, back to the old windmill.

Chapter 2

The next morning, as the cockerel sings his morning song, and Jack the chocolate Labrador sits under the big oak at the top of the hill, all the pedigree puppies get ready for the journey ahead. Wendy has tears of joy in her eyes and is as proud as can be. Burton, our very spirited, tail-chasing puppy, walks up to her and says, "I'm sorry for not being what you would wish me to be."

Wendy puts her paw around Burton and hugs him. "You could not be any more than you are, and that is all I wish from you. I love you for that. Only you can be what you are, and only you can become what you will. Now go on, and become all you can."

She smiles, and Burton smiles back. He bounces confidently over towards the other puppies.

Back on the other side of the stream, by the old windmill, Monkey is reaching for something. He stands on his back legs and stretches his front paws out as high as he can, with all his effort. Just above his front paws is a big tin. He pushes it and it starts to wobble. Slowly but surely, he gets it wobbling more and more until it falls sideways, hits the shelf, and the lid flips off. Paint starts to spill down out of the tin, like a black waterfall.

Monkey stands right underneath it and closes his eyes and his mouth. His whole body starts to go pure black. Soon the last glug of paint drops out onto his head. Slowly, he opens one eye and then the other. He turns around and runs up the old stairs at the side of the windmill, leaving little black paw prints along the way.

As the big fans of the mill turn round and round in the wind, Monkey stands tall and gets a full blast of air every time one of them passes him. Like a big hair dryer, the windmill slowly dries the paint. Monkey has now transformed himself into a stunning black Labrador puppy.

Outside the big red barn across the stream, all the puppies are sitting in a line waiting to get into the limousine, which will take them to Puppy School. One by one, they pass their mother, who leans down to

give them a good-luck kiss. Just as she bends to say goodbye to Burton, Monkey sneaks behind them and into the car, after which he is followed by Burton. Now, all inside the long limousine, the puppies wave goodbye to their mother out of the windows. Wendy – with Jack, who has now come down from the hill – watch the car drive away.

Inside the car, all the dogs sit up straight with pride. The long-awaited journey to Puppy School has begun. Right at the back, Monkey sits as upright as he can, looking a little awkward. All the others, including Burton, look at him strangely. But he just focuses straight ahead and holds in his excitement for the start of his adventure to Puppy School.

After about an hour, as all the puppies sleep, Burton watches eagerly out the front window of the car as it turns off the road. There in front of him is Puppy School – a huge old building with ten tall columns that stand like giants holding up the big, triangular roof.

A big stairway leads from the large wooden front doors, down to the driveway, which winds past a lake and many hedges cut into shapes of dogs. There is an adventure course with tires, ladders, tunnels, and see-saws. Burton barks to wake the others up. Slowly they open their eyes and stretch. As the limo drives up the long driveway, everyone looks out the windows. Burton and Monkey are next to each other, just taking it all in and smiling with wonder and excitement.

Chapter 3

Waiting on the steps is Perry, the principal, a very old and wise Irish wolfhound with a regal posture like a marble statue. Next to him is Miss Michelle, a very, sleek, slim, French Afghan hound from Paris. She is to teach the puppies in petiquette, a pedigree dog form of human etiquette, which will teach them how to behave, stand, eat, and bark. She has taught puppies for years at the school and has always been liked for her fair and kind ways.

The limo pulls up and the door opens. The puppies all jump out and sit tall and straight like puppy soldiers. Monkey sits right at the far end of the line. But he seems to be a little off with his sitting posture. Burton turns and looks at him, then he leans over and whispers in Monkey's ear. Monkey pulls in his rear, lifts his chin and sits tall and correct just like all the others. Burton gives Monkey a wink.

Principal Perry stands at the front of the line of puppies. "Welcome to Puppy School. My name is

Principal Perry. Follow me in single file, nice and straight, and keep in step. On the left paw, left paw walk."

All the puppies follow Perry, each trying ever so hard to keep in line and in step. Miss Michelle follows from behind. As she moves, her long hair floats from side to side as if in slow motion – like a hypnotic wave. Up the stairs they go and into the big, open entrance, which leads to a wonderful wooden corridor with cabinets evenly spaced along it. As they march past, Perry slows down a little so the puppies can take in all the pictures of other proud students, as well as all the golden bones and silver ball awards that the school has won over time. As they turn a corner into another corridor, Monkey sees a picture of a special looking dog, a golden Retriever. His picture glows with pride.

"Wow, who's he?" Monkey asks Miss Michelle.

She seems to melt as she looks at the photo. "Oh, that's Percy. One of the finest students puppy school has ever had. Not only a number-one student, but a remarkable dog in every way." Miss Michelle has gone all dreamy.

All of a sudden Burton, who is at the back of the line, lets out a loud whisper for them to hear. " Pssst!" Miss Michelle snaps out of her little dream and realizes that she and Monkey are now drifting apart from the others.

"Quickly," she tells Monkey.

As fast as he can, he scurries after the puppies, with Miss Michelle blushing behind him. But the floor is so well polished and slippery that when Monkey catches up to the marching line and tries to slow down, he slides into Burton, knocking him off his feet and into the next puppy, which causes a domino effect of puppies sliding into other puppies, until the first one in the line bumps into Perry. Silence. You could hear a pin drop. Perry stops. He turns his head smoothly and slowly. All he can see is a line of puppies squashed into each other. He looks at Miss Michelle, who starts to blush on top of her blush. Perry clears his throat, turns around, and continues. The puppies all follow. Monkey looks back at Miss Michelle and she smiles at him, as if to say, "Oops."

The next day, the puppies are all playing out on the gravel yard at the back of Puppy School. There is a wide staircase, which leads down to a big lawn with a long line of hedges. In the middle is a fountain. The puppies all stop playing as Miss Michelle glides out of the building and onto the gravel patio. They scurry to attention in a nice neat line. Monkey, of course, takes a little extra time to find his posture. Rear in, chin up.

Miss Michelle clears her throat. She starts to walk along the line of puppies, and speaks in her wonderful French accent. "You cannot buy class, but you can train to become classy. You can learn to have petiquette. You must learn to have good petiquette if you wish to be accepted into the world of Pedigree."

One of the puppies, which is a wonderful light golden color, raises her paw. Miss Michelle looks at her. This is Jazmin, the prettiest of all the puppies.

Miss Michelle nods, as if to say – go ahead, speak.

"Is it true that Pedigree dogs are better than other dogs, no matter what?"

Miss Michelle thinks for a second. Then she answers. "Every dog is equal. We are all dogs. Simple.

We all have our place in life. Some are meant for bigger things, and some not; but we are all part of a larger picture. Think of it like a jigsaw puzzle. Even the plain blue pieces of the sky or green bits of grass are just as important as the detailed part of the picture. What would you do if there were no mutts? Would you wish to do hard work and labor?

"No, I— um. No, I could not imagine being anything but a pedigree. It is all I've expected," Jazmin replies.

"Do you think a mutt might also expect to become a pedigree?" says Miss Michelle.

All the puppies start to laugh. One of them – Charles, a black Labrador – starts to pretend to be a mutt. He grimaces his face, slouches, and says in a deep, broken, accent, "I is gonna make somethin' of me. I is gonna learn me some class and teach me some petiquette and become a pedigree!"

All the pups laugh even louder. Miss Michelle looks at them with a little frown. Monkey feels a slight growl about to show, but suddenly he remembers he is supposed to be a pedigree. He pretends to laugh with all the others. Burton looks at Miss Michelle and sees it is not good behavior. He nudges Charles, who also notices Miss Michelle is not amused or the slightest bit happy. One by one, the pups nudge each other and stop laughing. Of course, the last one left is Monkey, who has now gone too far with trying to cover up his mutt anger and is laughing as loud as he can. Everyone watches him. Monkey suddenly feels all the eyes, and – just like a toy running out of batteries – his laughs get slower, and quieter, and slower, and even quieter . . . until silenced. Monkey has, yet again, put his foot in it.

"Mocking those who know no better and who can't help what they are born into is not the true essence of a pedigree," said Miss Michelle firmly and finally, making the message loud and clear. "You must NEVER look down on others. You have been blessed by birth, and you have the luck of a secured future. There have been many famous mutts who have earned respect from the pedigree world. So, find a place to bury that mocking bone of yours and be grateful of who you are, and never abuse others."

Just as she finishes speaking, a few raindrops start to fall. She looks up. "OK, we shall continue this class in the main hall. Form a line and follow me."

All the puppies, now with their tails between their legs in shame, jump into line and walk behind their teacher. Monkey, of course, is trying his best to walk like a pedigree. Burton is behind Monkey at the back of the line and just as the rain starts to become heavier he notices a small patch on Monkey's back start to drip and turn white. Then, another drip and it turns brown. The paint is starting to wash off.

Luckily, there is no one behind Burton, so he quickly tries to get Monkey's attention.

"Pssst," Burton calls. But Monkey puts his chin up even higher and pretends he cannot hear. Again, Burton makes a sound to get his attention, but this time Miss Michelle hears and she stops. All the puppies stop behind her. As Monkey stops and begins to turn around to see what Burton wants, Burton quickly reacts. He sticks his paw in some mud and wipes it on the white and brown patch of Monkey's back, smearing the wet paint with mud to cover it up.

Miss Michelle turns to look at him, pauses, and then turns back to marching.

"What are you doing? Why did you mess with my fur?" Monkey whispers.

"I think the rain was washing away your secret," Burton replies, and gives him a knowing look.

Oh, no! Monkey thinks. The truth is out. He will either be sent back to the farm or, even worse, to Muttly Manor: the prison pound for reject pedigrees and other dogs.

But Burton calms Monkey's fears. "You look out for me, and I'll look out for you. OK, pal?"

Monkey smiles. He has a new pedigree friend.

Chapter 4

The next day, all the puppies are training on the Adventure Course. There are ladders, slides, tunnels, and a dreaded seesaw. One by one, with a ten second break between each puppy, they rush off and start the course. Burton is first, then Charles, and then Monkey.

When Burton gets to the seesaw, he stops. He is gripped with fear. As he steps forward, the plank starts to fall, which makes him back up. By now, Charles has caught up with him and is getting impatient and even calling him names. Monkey is right behind Charles and is not happy that his friend is being teased. Burton is just about to make it across when Charles steps on the other end of the plank, making it wobble, and Burton slips. But he manages to pull himself back up.

As Charles laughs and steps backwards, Monkey steps aside to reveal a rock which Charles trips over, causing him to fall into a muddy puddle. Burton starts to laugh as Monkey quickly jumps onto the seesaw and scrambles across. As he gets to the other side, they both watch Charles slip and slide out of the mud and try to climb onto the seesaw. They let out a proud bark and run off to continue the course.

Both of them are now in a race – through the tunnel, up the ladder, down the slide, through a series of hoops all in a row, and then across the finish line. It's impossible to tell who won.

Sitting at the finish is the all-knowing Principal Perry. He just looks at them both with what could be the tiniest of smiles. The puppies had been told that nothing gets past the principal, which of course makes Monkey very nervous.

A week later, after many classes and lots of training and learning, the dogs are all outside at the back of the school, running around the dog-shaped hedges and enjoying some playtime. Burton is looking for Monkey, but can't seem to find him. Then, out of the door by the side of the school, he swiftly sneaks out.

"Where have you been?" Burton asks.

"Don't worry, you will soon find out." Monkey replies with a knowing smile.

Then, from out of the back door comes Miss Michelle. "OK, boys and girls, time for petiquette class!"

All the dogs stop what they are doing and rush into a line right by Miss Michelle. She turns and dreamily walks inside, with the proud pups behind her. Charles of course is always the first in the line, like the teachers pet. As they walk towards the class, Burton whispers to Monkey.

" What's going on?"

"Watch and see," says Monkey

Normally when they arrive at the classroom Miss Michelle waits for them all to get in the room and sit down. Of course Charles is always the first puppy to go in. As they get to the door, she turns and says. "Today we are going to try something new. I will go into the room, and you will all enter one at a time, as if entering into your human's house. " At this, a look of horror crosses Monkey's face, but it's too late. As Charles steps aside and sits, Miss Michelle walks into the room. It's like everything went into slow motion. Burton turns from Monkey to watch what he is watching, to see Miss Michelle open the door and a water balloon falls right onto her head. SPLASH! All the puppies start to laugh, but it is short lived as Perry appears from behind them. There is total silence. He looks at Miss Michelle. He just stands rigid, says nothing, and looks at all the puppies. All of their heads now hanging low in shame. Miss Michelle is trying to hold herself without embarrassment.

All the puppies are now standing in a line, and Principal Perry stands in front of them. "I want whoever did this to own up. If no one does, then you will all suffer the punishment."

Monkey knows it's the end of the road for him. He can't let everyone take the blame and be punished. Just as he is about to step forward, his good friend Burton steps out of the line. "It was me. Sorry, sir."

Principal Perry gives Burton a deeply angry look. Then he turns to walk out of the room, and shouts in a stern and strict voice, "Be outside my office in five minutes."

All the other puppies look at Burton with sympathy. Monkey can't believe what his friend did for him. "I'll help you with whatever the punishment is. I promise. I swear on it," he whispers, as he crosses his heart with his paw.

All the puppies walk past Burton and wish him good luck.

Chapter 5

That evening, Monkey sits with all the other puppies waiting for news of Burton. Suddenly, they hear some noise in the yard outside. Monkey rushes to the window. It's Burton. He's being put into the back of a small truck. All the other puppies are now squashed up to the window, watching.

"Oh no! He's going to Muttly Manor," says Charles.

Monkey runs out of the room, down the stairs, and manages to sneak out into the yard just as the truck is pulling away. He leaps onto the back step above the rear bumper. Burton is looking out of the window, with Monkey facing him, as all the other pups watch it drive off into the distance.

"I'll get you out of here. It's all my fault!" Monkey calls through the back window of the truck. Burton smiles as best he can through his worry.

Monkey rides with him, on the back, for about half an hour, until they drive up to a fenced-off broken down house. This is the famous Muttly Manor. It's a

large and slim, dark-gray, wooden house with some of the windows boarded up. The curtains are all ripped and dirty, and everything looks like it's about to fall apart. Black sooty smoke pours out of a broken brick chimney. The truck pulls up outside the large wire fence that surrounds the house just as a milk truck is leaving. Monkey notices It's the same one that goes to Puppy School.

He jumps off just before the driver comes to get his friend out, and hides behind one of the back tires. Burton is taken into a gate and shut in the yard full of broken metal, old furniture, and a few old trucks with no wheels. There is junk everywhere. Monkey sneaks around to the side where he can talk through the fence.

"I'll come back before sunrise in the morning and we can start to work on a plan. Be strong. Hold your head high. No matter how frightened you are, you must show strength. If you show weakness you will be a target for bullies," Monkey says, giving Burton his best mutt-advice.

"You have to go back. The final exams are in a few days, and you can't get caught!" says Burton.

"You look out for me, and I'll look out for you." Monkey winks, turns, and runs off. He manages to catch up to the milk truck stopped at some lights. He hops onto the back just as it starts to moves away.

Back at Muttly Manor, Burton turns around to see the full view of his new home. It's real rough. Old, leaky, broken, wooden doghouses are dotted around the yard. Soggy blankets and moldy scraps of food are just lying here and there. In the corner is a big Boxer-Pitt bull mutt. This is Cowboy. He's a dirty, golden color with a wonderful brown and white streak running from his head, down his face, and around his eye to his nose.

"Whatcha lookin' at posh kid?" he says in a deep, growling New York accent.

Burton gets up to walk past him, but Cowboy jumps up and snaps, growls and barks, until the rope he is attached to pulls tight. Monkey's words about staying strong ring in his head.

As Burton moves towards one of the broken dog-houses, a small, brown-and-white Mexican Chihuahua-mutt comes out. This is Little. He bites the nails of one paw and then licks the other and tries to flatten a tuft of hair sticking up on top of his head. All the while, he rambles on in a Mexican broken English accent. "I don't know man. I don't know. Oh man. Not another one. How long he gonna last, man? Oh dude, you pure pedigree. Wow!" He licks his paw again and tries to flatten the tuft of hair, but it just springs back as it was before. "I need to gets me a hair cut or somethin, man. This is driving me crazy. I don't know, man. I mean, I should be in Mexico with my cousins. I don't know how, what, where or when, man."

He is obviously a dog full of worries and slightly neurotic; as in, highly strung; as in, his speed dial has been turned right up to full, and then some. Burton finds a corner and manages to move a blanket to find a dry spot. He curls up to try and sleep. Suddenly, loud sounds of pots and pans, and a man grumbling and rambling loudly, can be heard from inside Muttly

Manor. Both Cowboy and Little seem to be very scared and they both curl up and pretend to be asleep.

Chapter 6

The next day, before sunrise, Monkey hops off the milk cart and makes his way towards Muttly Manor. "Psst!" he whispers as loud as he can, trying not to wake the rest of the house. "Pssssst, Burton!"

This time it works. Burton wakes, and sees his good friend. He gets up, stretches, and then rushes over to the fence. As he passes by, Cowboy leaps up and jumps for him, but again his rope snaps tight and Cowboy just barks and growls. Burton manages to get by and reach the fence, where he can talk face to face with Monkey.

"What are we going to do?" Burton asks. "I'm frightened this big guy is going to get me."

Monkey looks at Cowboy, who is now standing and just growling at them. He leans in to whisper to Burton. "You see how the grass around him is worn out in a half moon shape?" Burton turns to see what Monkey is talking about. "That's as far as he can go. The rope stops him going anywhere outside that half moon. He has worn down the grass in his rope range. So, as long as you are a yard in front of that line, he can't get to you. Stand your ground and when the rope goes tight just bark as loudly and as ferociously as you can. I bet that will put the bully in his place."

Burton looks back again and sees the trodden down and dirty half moon shape-surrounding Cowboy. He smiles nervously.

"I have a plan to get you out," says Monkey, "but it will have to be early tomorrow. I have to get back for some final training for the exam. It's the heelwork, walking with a human by my side. But I'm having a problem getting it right. I've never done heel work before."

Now it's Burton's turn to give Monkey some advice. "My mum told me about this once. It can be quite hard, but she told me the secret to making it fun and easy. When you walk next to your owner, you are supposed to be looking forward, with your head high, not at them. But somehow you still have to know when they move and turn, right?"

Monkey nods. "That's what I can't get. If they move and I am not looking, I get stepped on, or sometimes I go the wrong way and I step on them." He sounds a little frustrated.

"The trick is to keep your eye – the one closest to the leg next to you – on the tips of the feet only. When your owner changes direction, his shoe tips will point to the direction that he or she is going. The first sign of a turn is the tips of the shoes. Then you can react and move with them. Just keep the corner of your eye on the corner of the shoe closest to you."

Monkey thinks about this. He does a little walk with his head held high, keeping one eye a little to one side – but he starts to go cross-eyed. He stops and shakes his head.

Burton laughs. "It's only a tiny look to the side, like catching a slice of their toes. You'll get it with practice."

Monkey walks along the fence again, and Burton follows, watching his eye. Again, Monkey shakes his head and tries to start over. Suddenly, there is a loud crashing noise from inside the house. Little scurries across the yard screaming in Mexican, and Cowboy jolts up and backs into his corner like a wimp.

"I'll be back in the morning to get you out. Remember, keep out of the half moon and he can't touch you." whispers Monkey as fast as he can. Then he runs off into the field as Burton turns and runs into a broken doghouse. Cowboy peers out of his corner, and Little's nose and eyes stick out of a rusty paint tin. Burton slowly comes out of the doghouse. It's quiet again.

Little starts rambling on and walks around in circles. "Oh, man. That crazy man. Oh man. He's, like, full of loco, man. He's like the devil. Oh, man, my nerves can't take this. "

All of a sudden, a grumbling sound comes from Burton's belly. He hasn't eaten for nearly a whole day. He turns around and sees the food bowl and scraps are right next to the half moon line. This is it, he thinks to himself. He stands tall and gets ready to face Cowboy – but no, he decides against it and steps back.

But again his stomach calls to him. He tries to quiet it with his paw, but it continues to grumble. He looks over at Cowboy, takes a deep breath, and moves towards the edge of the half moon. Little, shivering and chewing on his nails, watches nervously through one open eye.

Burton gets about a yard away from the bowl and scraps and leans forward to sniff. Pow! Cowboy jumps up like he has been fired from a slingshot. The rope snaps tight, and he is snarling and barking, hanging half in the air, with his front paws outstretched. Burton jumps back, but sees that Cowboy has hit the limit line of the half moon.

Burton takes another deep breath. He is only a yard away, right in front of Cowboy. He lets out his biggest, loudest, angriest bark. Little shoots back into his paint tin and Cowboy suddenly drops to all four paws with a stunned expression. Burton stands strong and tall. Then, without a bark or a snarl, like a switch had turned night into day, Cowboy backs away.

Burton moves even closer. "What's your problem?" Burton asks. "Why do you have to be so angry?"

Cowboy just looks at Burton.

Little has now come out of his tin and is standing behind Burton, feeling all tough and proud with his new buddy. "Yeah, man. Why you gotta keep frightening me, man. I don't want no trouble, man," he squeaks. Then he swallows a very large, dry, nervous swallow, and steps one-step back to safety.

They both wait. Cowboy lifts his shamed head. "I'm scared! So I just think, if I'm scary, then no ones gonna hurt me, you know? Everyone has always been horrible to me."

Cowboy is a big dopey, softy. Just another bully who does not wish to be bullied, and so takes it out on others.

"I don't want to hurt you," Burton says. "I just want to be friends with you and with Little. We're stuck in here together. My mum always said that there's no need to make enemies. We should all help each other, not fight."

Little moves up to Burton and puts his skinny little leg and paw on Burton's shoulder. "Yeah, man. We just want peace, man. Just peace. That's all," says a now very confident and less stressed Little.

Cowboy nods his head. "I'm sorry," he says softly.

All of a sudden, there is a loud shout from in the house, followed by sounds of things being broken. Little scampers back into his paint tin so fast it starts to roll and roll until it hits the wall. Cowboy hides in his corner and Burton is left standing. He is frozen in fear.

The man comes bursting out the back door. He is really tall, with a big belly and grey balding hair that grows wildly in all directions. He has a grey beard and wears a dirty old t-shirt, blue, ripped up work overalls, and big boots with no laces.

"All I need is another posh puppy on my hands," the man says all gruffly, as he tries to kick Burton. "You pedigree good-for-nothing! Think ya something,' hey? I'll have you eatin' dirt from now on." He kicks the bowl, and all the food goes flying over the yard.

"We'll see how tough you are. You're going to my cousin's tomorrow. You think I'm bad. Ha! He was born and raised with the devil, and drinks all day with him, too!" He tries once more to kick Burton, but again Burton ducks and dives away. Frustrated, the man picks up a can and throws it towards him. It just misses his head and bounces off the floor and into the tin where Little is hiding. The man grunts, groans something under his breath and goes inside. Little stumbles out of his tin with a ringing in his ears, and his eyes rolling around in his head. Cowboy is frozen where he is, terrified. He looks at his new friend – who might not be his new friend for long.

"My pal Monkey will get us out tomorrow. I know it. I promise. This time tomorrow, we will be free," Burton tells him. But Little and Cowboy do not believe in their new friend so quickly. They know how dangerous the man is. And how impossible it is to get out.

Chapter 7

The next morning just before sunrise, on the hill over-looking Sunnyfields farm, Jack lies under the oak tree. He opens his eyes, and he breathes in a nice, deep breath of morning air. He gets up and has a long stretch. Crack! The sound of a twig snaps behind him. He turns slowly to see Monkey standing there. They look at each other. There is a funny silence.

Then Monkey just blurts it out. "I need your help. My friend is in Muttly Manor and I need to get him out, I don't know who else to ask."

"Muttly Manor?" Jack asks quietly. He shakes his head, as a deep frown appears. He obviously knows something about this place.

Monkey continues to plead with Jack, rambling on about Puppy School and the prank gone wrong and how Burton took the blame. Suddenly, Jack lets out a loud bark. Monkey stops his desperate story in shock.

"Maybe, if you stop talking, we could actually start to do something about it and get your buddy out,"

Jack says nice and calmly. He smiles at Monkey. "Follow me"

Jack leads the way, and Monkey continues to ramble on. "I've got to help him and get back to Puppy School for my test in the morning," says Monkey.

"You managed to stay the distance then? I'm amazed," says Jack.

Monkey is confused. "How did you know?"

Jack stops and looks at Monkey. "I sit up here and see all. I saw you slip into the limo. Oh, and nice paint job."

Monkey doesn't know what to say.

Jack turns with a smile and starts to run. "Keep up, pedigree mutt."

An hour later at Muttly Manor, Burton sits with Cowboy as Little walks up to them complaining in his crazy language about the food, the wet, and how he wishes he was in sunny Mexico. Suddenly, Cowboy spots someone coming over the ridge. It's Jack and Monkey.

Burton quickly moves to the fence where the others meet him. There is a lot of whispering between Jack,

Burton, and Monkey, while Cowboy and Little sit nervously, waiting to hear the escape plan. Burton goes to the back door of the house and Jack runs around the side of the fence and starts to dig. After a minute or so the earth just sinks. He uncovers an entrance to a small tunnel. Monkey is shocked.

"Let's just say I used this a long time ago for my own escape," says Jack.

He hunches down and crawls into the tunnel. Monkey sits nervously on the outside of the fence and Cowboy, Burton, and Little excitedly wait on the inside. Suddenly, next to the big water tower, the ground starts to move, and Jack comes bursting through. He shakes the dirt off his head, and turns to Monkey, who quickly jumps into the tunnel and comes out on the inside.

"We have to get my friends out," says Burton.

Monkey smiles at the new bond his pedigree friend has made with the rough kids. They are somehow going to have to cut through the thick rope that holds Cowboy. Monkey and Burton look at the rope, then at each other. They both put their heads down and start working at it, chewing away with their sharp puppy teeth as if the rope was corn on the cob.

Jack walks up to a very nervous Little and opens his jaws wide. Little stops chewing his nails, and puts his paws over his eyes. "I don't want to die," he shouts. SNAP! Jack's jaws close on the smaller rope attached to Little. He's free. Little is so relieved that he jumps around and licks Jack like crazy. Jack accepts his wet thanks with a smile. But Little is so over-enthusiastic that he knocks over a metal can, which hits a shovel, which comes crashing down onto the hard yard floor. Everyone freezes. Silence.

Suddenly, they hear a sound from inside the house. "Oh, no. The man is coming out." Burton whispers. Little hides his rope under himself to cover it up, and lies down. He is so nervous, he shakes almost four times as hard as he normally does, which makes his teeth chatter like castanets. Burton runs to the hole and tries to cover it up, and Monkey and Jack hide behind some trashcans. Just as Monkey manages to tuck himself away, the man bursts out of the back door, but this time he is carrying a big double-barreled shotgun.

"What is going on with you good-for-nothin', no-good, hairy mutts?"

Everyone is still. Cowboy sees his half-chewed rope and leans on it, pretending to be asleep. The man sees the shovel on the ground and walks towards it. Then, out of the corner of his eye, he sees something move near the trashcans. It's Monkey's tail.

"Who's there?" he shouts angrily.

He lifts and aims the gun as he walks slowly towards them. Cowboy watches. He has to do something. He looks at Burton. Burton looks down at the half moon around Cowboy and sees that the man is nearly out of range.

The man sees Monkey hiding and points the gun right at him. Suddenly, Jack steps out, and puts himself between Monkey and the gun.

The man steps back. He seems to recognize Jack. "What the—? You? How did you get back in here?"

Cowboy sees the man is now about one inch out of range. He chews frantically on the half-chewed rope.

Jack starts to growl. And it's a vicious, frightening, deep growl. He moves towards the man. The man fearfully steps back into the half moon. He is now in range. It's Cowboy's only chance. The man aims the gun at Jack. Burton looks at Cowboy desperately. That's it. Cowboy finds the courage to overcome his fear, and he leaps full-pounce with a thunderous bark.

The man spins around as Cowboy lands on him and the rope snaps tight. But it quickly creaks and cracks under the strain, which snaps him free, and he takes the man down to the ground knocking the gun out of his hand. Cowboy courageously growls and barks at him. Little is now running around in circles, rambling away. He bounces off a trashcan, spins around, and looks at the man on the ground. He growls, turns around, lifts his leg, and does a wee on the man's shoulder as he smiles defiantly.

Burton rushes to the great-escape hole with Monkey, then Little, and then Jack. The man pushes Cowboy off him and grabs for his gun. Just before he goes through the hole, Jack turns to see the man aim the gun at Cowboy. He turns around and leaps as quick

and as fast as he can landing on the man's back with his front paws. BANG! The gun goes off.

All the dogs look. Cowboy doesn't move. Burton runs to see if his buddy is OK, but the man has turned around and aims the gun at him. Burton growls a little puppy growl. He tries to bite the man's feet. The man takes aim, but Burton moves too fast around and around his feet and his ankles. Jack jumps again, this time he knocks the man down and the gun flies out of his hands, again. Jack stands over him with fangs showing and growls like a wild wolf. Burton looks at his new hero in awe. To the side Cowboy struggles to his feet. He's a little shaken, but OK.

"Get out, all of you. Go!" Jack barks to them.

One by one, the escape continues as Jack stands over the frightened man. Little, Burton, Monkey, and Cowboy now all stand on the other side of the fence and watch helplessly. Can Jack make it? Jack looks at the hole then he snaps and barks as if to bite the man. The man curls into a ball in fear. It's Jack's moment. He turns around and leaps to the tunnel at the speed of lightning. The man uncurls, scrambles up, and finds his gun. He turns.

But it's too late. All the dogs are running off into the distance.

Chapter 8

The next morning, as the sun is about to peek over the horizon, Monkey sneaks back into puppy school as the gang watches. He stops and turns to look at his friends. Jack gives him a wink, Burton raises a paw, and Cowboy raises his head with pride and courage. Little stands on his back paws, waving both front paws and rambling on about how he could have been a contender at Puppy School. They all laugh as Monkey sneaks through a hedge.

That morning Puppy School is as busy as can be. The day of the finals has arrived. The exams into pedigreedom had created great tension.

Outside, Monkey sits in a line with all the other puppies. He sits like a bold statue. Principal Perry walks out with Miss Michelle and, one by one, each of the pups are called away to go through the final tests.

First there is the walking and obedience, followed by petiquette. Then the final adventure assault course. All the pups sit tall and watch, as one by one, they are taken through the tests. Everyone is supporting each other and there is nothing but good will.

Each time a puppy finishes the tests, they are walked past the others who are waiting, and sit in a line opposite them. Slowly but surely, the line on one side gets longer with finished contestants, and the line on the other side gets shorter.

Next up is Charles and then finally it's Monkey. Both Puppies look at each other nervously.

"Good luck. I know you have what it takes to be great," says Monkey.

Charles smiles and gives a confident thank you nod.

Monkey sits and watches, his stomach in knots from nerves and hunger. Charles is doing well. He sails through the walking and obedience and is pure pedigree when it comes to petiquette. The final test is the adventure course. Some of the other puppies that have finished give a cheer to help him on his way. The whistle is blown and off he goes.

Now everything seems to go in slow motion for Monkey. He has managed to stay the whole duration and get to a point that no other mutt has ever dared.

His dream is now only moments away from becoming a reality. He watches as Charles flies through the course. He nearly falls on the seesaw, but recovers well. He speeds through the tires and the tunnel, leaps up the ladder to the top and, without even hesitating, jumps down and crosses the finish line, where he takes a proud sitting position. Miss Michelle walks over and Charles follows her to the end of the line opposite Monkey.

"Well done," she whispers to Charles. She turns and looks at Monkey. He sits with the posture of a true pedigree. She nods, and Monkey follows her to the start of the test. Now everyone's eyes are on him. Even from the edge of the field, Cowboy, Little, Burton, and Jack's heads all peek through a hedge, watching nervously.

First up, it's the walking test. Monkey walks with such ease it looks as if he is in slow motion. His is head high, tail straight, and he has a perfect stride. As he gets to the end of the walk, he stops, turns around, and sits tall. Chin up, rear in. He looks proud and confident. Miss Michelle looks at Principal Perry, who gives her a slight nod, but that's it. He is like an officer in the army: no emotion shows through.

Next is the dreaded heel walk. Miss Michelle walks up to Monkey. She stands next to him and he gets up and stands tall next to her. She turns her head slightly and gives a warm smile to help ease his nerves. Off she strides. Burton's words are ringing in Monkey's head now. The corner of his eye is focused on Miss Michelle's paws as he looks forward and strides tall. She takes a sudden left turn, and with a slight hesitation Monkey quickly manages to take a longer stride and keep up to her. Principal Perry looks on stone-faced. Now she takes a right turn. This time Monkey is more comfortable and relaxed. As Miss Michelle turned, Monkey turned, almost as if they were one. The perfect heel! Then another left turn. Then a long straight walk with no turns.

Back at the hedge, Burton wishes with all his heart that his friend can keep his wonderful performance going. Two more left turns, two right turns, one long straight walk, and then they come to a sudden stop. Both Monkey and Miss Michelle sit proud. There is a bark from the hedge. Everyone turns to see who it came from, but there is no one there. Behind the hedge, Jack sits smiling as Cowboy, Little, and Burton all giggle with paws over their mouths. Meanwhile Monkey sits with a small smile. He knows whose bark that was.

Miss Michelle walks over to Principal Perry and sits tall and fantastically beautiful. Her long hair flows like waves in the wind. Principal Perry walks up to Monkey. All the other puppies sit tall and watch nervously. Jack, Burton, Cowboy and little have their heads peering through the hedge again.

The next two stages are the easiest for Monkey. He sails through obedience and pettiquette effortlessly. He now feels he is where he always thought he could be and would be. The little mutt who could, is. Now Principal Perry stands back as Miss Michelle leads Monkey over to the final part of his exam: the adventure assault course.

Monkey stands at the ready. The sound of a whistle echoes loudly around Puppy School. Like a bullet from a gun, Monkey shoots off towards the first obstacle.

Barks and cheers come from the hedge and from all the other puppies. Everyone wants him to do well. Monkey flies up a ramp and leaps off into a sand pit. He struggles with his grip, but finally gets out and rushes towards the seesaw.

Now, there is quiet everywhere. Monkey has the determination of a hero. He leaps onto the lower end of the seesaw and bounds across. Even as it tips, he continues like a gymnast along the slim board. SMASH! The other end shudders as it hits the ground, and Monkey leaps off and continues towards the line of tires. One leap in and one out, tire after tire. It's like he has springs in his paws. Not a hitch. A perfect score. He leaps out of the last tire, switches direction, and heads for the tunnel. Whoosh, and he's out the other side. Now there is a small distance of running, then the tall ladder climb.

Burton, Jack, Cowboy, and Little have all leaned through the hedge so far that they fall through. They scramble up and continue to watch. Little is so nervous he has to watch through his paws, which are covering his eyes.

Monkey runs so fast to the ladder that he has to quickly slam on the brakes. But he can't stop in time and he slides in the dirt. Thud! Everyone gasps at the same time. Then silence. Perry is sitting tall, emotionless, just watching. Miss Michelle nearly runs forward to see if he is OK, but Monkey gets to his feet and shakes off the dirt from his face. He takes a few backward steps, hesitates for a second, looks up at the ladder, and then pounces onto it like a tiger.

He scrambles up each run with all his determination. At the top he looks down a little nervous, but he knows he has to just take the leap of faith. Again like a tiger, he leaps off. Not one dog dares to even breathe. Monkey is in the air for what seems to be an eternity. He lands and tumbles through the dirt, creating a dust cloud around him. No one can see him.

Then suddenly, out of the fog of dust, he bursts through. Cheers erupt from the hedge and also from the line of puppies. Miss Michelle desperately wants to join in, but she contains herself. But of course inside her head she is jumping for joy.

Monkey is in full gallop, running proud to the finish line. Principal Perry waits like a statue at the end for him. A tiny smile almost escapes from the side of his usually tightly closed mouth. Monkey sits under Principal Perry's head, huffing and panting, but still as regal as a pedigree. Perry looks down at him with a proud face. Monkey looks straight ahead as Miss Michelle comes to take him back to the line where all the other puppies are, then leads them back inside the school. "Well done all of you," she whispers in her wonderful French accent. "Get cleaned up, and we will have the award ceremony in an hour."

All the puppies are smiling but exhausted from all the excitement and tension.

Chapter 9

About an hour later, out on the back lawn of Puppy School, dogs of all pedigrees sit waiting in front of a stage, which has a podium and a desk with all the dogrees laid out in a line. Over to the left of the crowd is Wendy, who is standing with another Labrador who looks very much like Jack. Right at the back, staying hidden, are Jack, Burton, Cowboy and Little.

Miss Michelle exits the school with the puppies. They are all well groomed, as the sunshine glitters off their fur. Like soldiers, they follow her to the back of the podium. One at a time, they all sit down. Charlie and Monkey sit at the end. Monkey sits proud with his head held high. At the back, Burton climbs onto Jack's shoulders so he can see his buddy. Monkey sees him and smiles.

Principal Perry now walks out of the school. He is an amazing sight to behold. He strides like a king towards the podium. Everyone is quiet. He clears his throat, and says. "Today a new generation of puppies will move forward into the world to continue to live in the name and ways of pedigree. You are honored to be able to have this start in life. You must always be grateful and never feel as though you are better than any other because of your fortunate beginnings. To enter the world of pedigree is not a right; it is an honor you have earned."

Then, One by one, Principal Perry calls out the names of each puppy. And one by one they go up, and he picks up their dogree with his mouth and passes it to each student. Each time, cheers and barking erupt from the audience. The time has finally come. Monkey sits alone on the stage.

Principal Perry turns to him. "The last dogree belongs to a dog who I have been watching closely from the start. Monkey, come and claim what your hard work has earned."

The crowd erupts. Cowboy and Little whistle. Jack barks as loud as he can. Monkey walks up proudly, his smile as wide as his face. Miss Michelle is now crying openly. Monkey sits in front of Principal Perry awaiting his prize. But Perry sees something. He was just about to lean over and give Monkey his dogree, but he stops. He turns his head, puts the dogree back on the table, and looks at Monkey with a stony face. "I think someone is showing his true colors," he says.

Monkey slowly turns and sees that a big patch of his coloring has come off on his back legs. The game is up.

It's too late. A tear falls down Monkey's face. Principal Perry just looks knowingly at him. Everyone else is wondering what is happening. Suddenly, Monkey runs off the stage and leaps into the fountain nearby. He stands under the flowing water as his color starts to run. Gasps and cries of, "Mutt!" and "Fake!" come from the audience.

He steps out of the water and shakes. There he is, in all his colorful accident-in-a paint-factory glory. He jumps onto the stage. Everyone goes quiet.

"OK. So I'm not what I should be. I'm just a mutt. And because of that fact, I don't deserve to be here. But I just wanted the chance to make something of myself. To become as special as the pedigree dogs I always admired. Is that such a crime?"

The crowd is silent. Principal Perry is in shock.

Monkey sees Burton sitting on top of Jacks head. "I would never have made it this far if it wasn't for one special pedigree puppy who kept my secret and allowed me to show you all that even a mutt can earn a dogree. He took the blame for something I did and ended up in Muttly Manor."

Miss Michelle looks at Principal Perry, who is now a little confused.

Monkey continues. "He trained me, gave me advice, even from behind the fence of that terrible place. Even when he was suffering. So if anyone deserves this dogree, it is my dearest friend Burton – a true pedigree."

He jumps around Principal Perry and stands by the last dogree. "I hereby claim this dogree in the name of a true friend and true pedigree. A dog that sees everyone as equal. Burton, come and get your dogree." Monkey looks at Principal Perry, expecting him to step in and stop him. But Perry just sits and waits.

Burton is too frightened to go up. Slowly, getting louder and louder, the crowd shouts his name. "Burton! Burton! Burton!" He hides behind Jack but Jack turns to look at him. Burton knows he has to do the right thing and makes his way up to the stage. Wendy stands tall and feels very proud of her little boy. Burton makes his way and jumps up to be with his friend. For a moment Monkey and him just look at each other. Then they both turn to look at Perry, who now has a big smile on his face.

Jack, Cowboy, and Little have made their way up to the front and stand next to Wendy and the other Labrador.

Burton starts to speak. "I have learned that the quality of a dog has nothing to do with where he comes from. The quality of a dog comes from his decisions to do what is right and not be selfish. And to see that, no matter what the breeding, one dog is not better than another. We are all one of the same. We are dogs. And I would give up my pedigree again to keep my new friends that I have made in the last few days. I have seen courage and truth come from the heart and not from training. Not from trying to make

others happy. Monkey is a kind of pedigree I could only dream of being."

From the audience there is a mix of gasps of snobbery and also acceptance.

Principal Perry walks up to Burton. He looks down at him. There is silence. He turns to Monkey and looks at him. Both puppies stand to either side of Perry in front of everyone. Then Perry clears his throat and speaks. "After what I have heard and what I have seen, I hereby declare both Monkey and Burton equal degrees. Not only for their admirable qualities, but also for showing me what this school has avoided and ruled out, for far too long. No matter where a dog comes from, they are equal. And never again will this school keep its doors closed to the mutts of this world."

Suddenly, from behind them, Miss Michelle whoops three times and screams, " Yo Monkey the pedigree!" in a very loud, strong, New York, kind of street, accent. Again the audience falls silent. Perry is stunned. The puppies are stunned too.

Miss Michelle blushes. All eyes are on her. "OK, OK. Yeah, yeah. So I ain't no Frenchy," she says. "I'm just a plain Afghan girl from New York city. What can I say?"

Perry walks up to her. The puppies are dumbstruck. Their French lady turned out to be a working-class girl.

Perry stands next to her and shouts, "Vive la difference!"

The crowd barks and howls. Then, out of the middle of the crowd, Monkey's mother Harley walks out and towards the stage.

Monkey sees her and rushes up to greet her. "I'm sorry mum. I'm sorry."

She just shakes her head. "No, it's I who should be sorry. I told you we don't belong here. I told you we were not good enough. You proved to me, and to everyone else, that anything is possible no matter who you are. I'm so proud of you."

In the background, Little dances and jumps all over Cowboy and sings a song about going to Puppy

School. Wendy looks up at her little boy Burton on the stage as a tear falls down her face.

The Final Chapter

Early that evening, back at Sunnyfields Farm, all the dogs are enjoying the sunshine as they relax near the stream.

Monkey walks up to Jack and asks, "How come you knew about Muttly Manor?"

Before Jack speaks, Harley starts to tell the story. "That was where Jack was sent after a problem at Puppy School. He was always a bit of a loner. If it weren't for him, I would still be there too. He dug a tunnel for us to get out."

Monkey is a little confused.

"We came back here to live so Jack could be near his old family – his sister Wendy," says Harley. "So, you can thank your father for saving us both from Muttly Manor."

Monkey can't believe what he just heard. He is stunned.

"I've been keeping an eye on you from up on my hill," says Jack.

Suddenly Burton speaks up. "So, if you are my mum's brother, that means you are my uncle, and Monkey is my cousin?"

Monkey and Burton look at each other. They are more than equal. They are family.

"Hey cousin!" says Burton.

"See, I am pedigree after all," says Monkey.

"All dogs are mutts," says Jack. "The only pure dog and only true pedigree is the wild wolf. No matter what the breed, every other dog is a mix from that original. So we are all mutts."

Wendy smiles at this truth from Jack.

Monkey looks at Burton. "So, my cousin is a mutt?"

Burton leaps onto him and they roll around in the grass giggling. Jack walks over to give Wendy and Harley a kiss each, and then he wanders back up onto his hill to look over his territory. The sun shines on Sunnyfields farm as the boys run around the tall grass. Both Wendy and Harley sit and watch the pedigree mutts at play.

THE END